APR 29 2011

CAT SECRETS

Jef Czekaj

Balzer + Bray
An Imprint of HarperCollinsPublishers

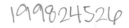

Balzer + Bray is an imprint of HarperCollins Publishers.

Cat Secrets
Copyright © 2011 by Jef Czekaj
All rights reserved. Manufactured in China.
No part of this book may be used or reproduced in any manner whatsoever without written permission except in the
case of brief quotations embodied in critical articles and reviews. For information address HarperCollins Children's Books,
a division of HarperCollins Publishers, 10 East 53rd Street, New York, NY 10022. www.harpercollinschildrens.com

Library of Congress Cataloging-in-Publication Data
Czekaj, Jef.
    Cat secrets / by Jef Czekaj. — 1st ed.
        p.   cm.
    Summary: Important secrets about how best to live a cat's life will be revealed only to those
who can prove that they are genuine cats.
    ISBN 978-0-06-192088-2 (trade bdg.)
    [1. Cats—Fiction.]   I. Title.   PZ7.C9987Cat 2011   [E]—dc22   2009049424   CIP   AC

Typography by Carla Weise
11   12   13   14   15   SCP   10   9   8   7   6   5   4   3   2   1
❖
First Edition

Okay, now that only cats are reading, we can begin.
The first Cat Secret is . . .
CAT SECRETS
CAT SECRETS
Wait! Wait!

It has come to my attention that someone other than a cat may be reading this book.

Shame on you.

Hey, you!
Yes, you!
You don't look much
like a cat!

Hmm. That was actually a pretty good "meow."
I guess they really are all cats.
ZZIP!
CAT SECRETS

I'm still not convinced. Let's hear them *purr*.

They'll never get that one!

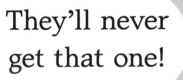

That sounded like a purr to me.

Me too.
I guess I'll start revealing our Cat Secrets.

ZZZiP!

Wait, I know!
Let's see them *stretch* like a kitty.

CAT SECRETS

If you *absolutely*,
really, *truly* are a cat,
let's see you take
a nap!

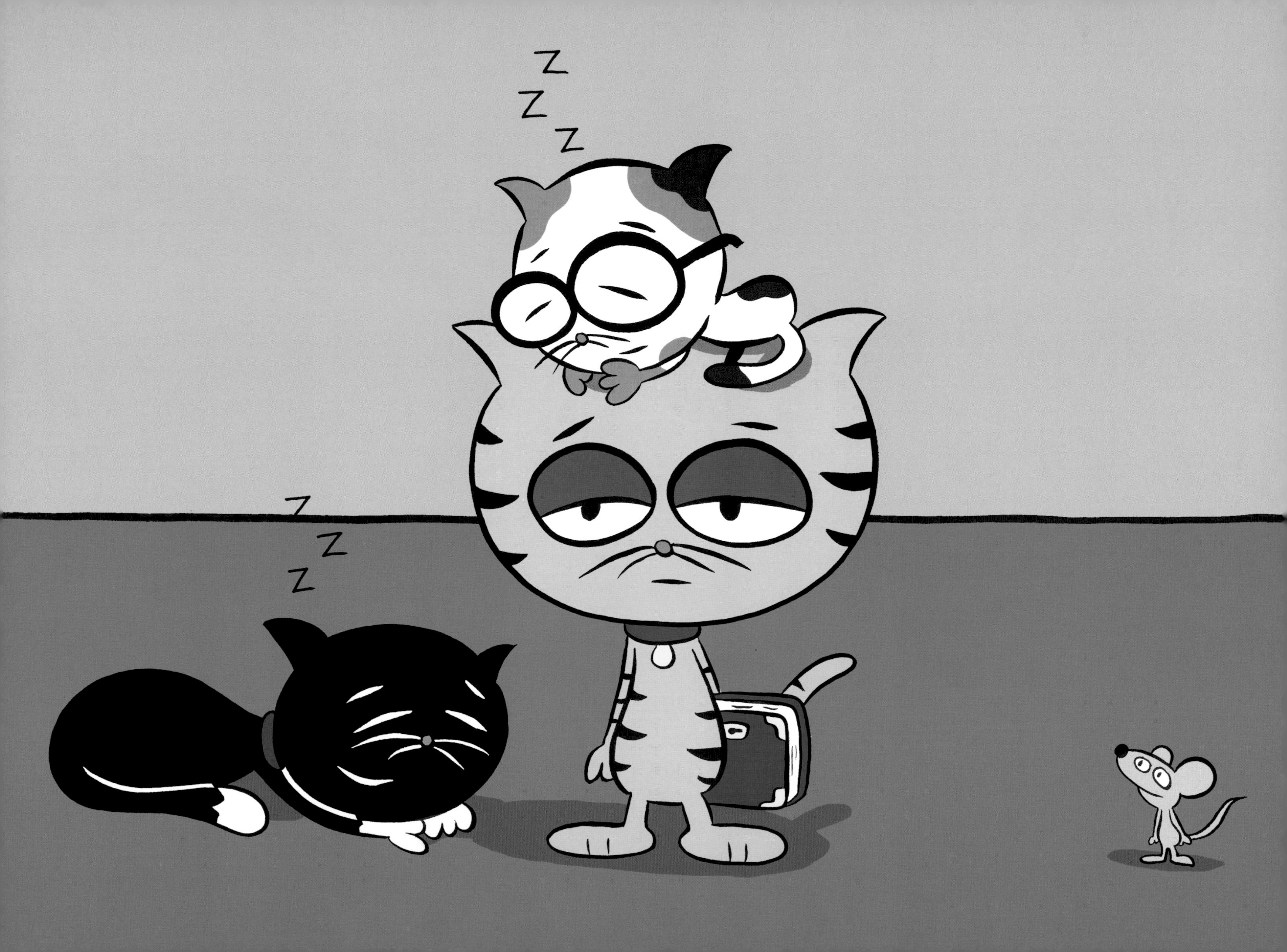
ZZZ
ZZZ